250

Y0-CBH-914

YOU NEVER EXPECTED YOUR DAY OFF TO TURN OUT LIKE THIS!

You're hiking to town when two men in a pickup offer you a ride. You know the rule . . . but what can happen on a short ride? Will you go with them or not?

The storm is getting worse. You need to get your rowboat to shore. Then you see a small girl, alone in a boat, calling for help. Can you save her? Should you try?

You wake up in a huge fishbowl—with a fish staring in at you. The fish is trying to talk to you! How did you get here? More to the point, how can you get out?

What happens in this book is up to you, according to the choices you make, page by page. You'll find over thirty possible endings, from silly to serious to surprising. And it all starts when you get up one beautiful summer morning . . .

Ask for these other Making Choices titles from Chariot Books

PROFESSOR Q'S MYSTERIOUS MACHINE
Donna Fletcher Crow

DR. ZARNOFF'S EVIL PLOT
Donna Fletcher Crow

MR. X'S GOLDEN SCHEME
Donna Fletcher Crow

THE HAWAIIAN COMPUTER MYSTERY
Janet Chester Bly

THE PRESIDENT'S STUCK IN THE MUD and Other Wild West Escapades, Stephen A. Bly

TROUBLE IN QUARTZ MOUNTAIN TUNNEL
Stephen A. Bly

A HORSE NAMED FUNNY BITS
Rose Marie Goble

THE CEREAL BOX ADVENTURES
Barbara Bartholomew

FLIGHT INTO THE UNKNOWN
Barbara Bartholomew

HELP! I'M DROWNING

(AND OTHER EMERGENCIES)

PEGGY DOWNING

Illustrated by Bruce Bulloch

from David C. Cook Publishing Co.

For
Douglas and Marlys

Chariot Books is an imprint of David C. Cook Publishing Co.

David C. Cook Publishing Co., Elgin, Illinois 60120
David C. Cook Publishing Co., Weston, Ontario
HELP! I'M DROWNING! (AND OTHER EMERGENCIES)
© 1985 by Peggy Downing
All rights reserved. Except for brief excerpts for review purposes, no part of this book may be reproduced or used in any form without written permission from the publisher.

Cover art and illustrations by Bruce Bulloch
First Printing, 1985
Printed in the United States of America
89 88 87 86 85 5 4 3 2 1

Library of Congress Cataloging in Publication Data

Downing, Peggy,
Help! I'm drowning! (and other emergencies).

Summary: A plot-it-yourself adventure story set in a mountain resort. The reader's decisions determine the outcome of the plot.
1. Plot-your-own stories. 2. Children's stories, American. [1. Plot-your-own stories. 2. Adventure and adventurers—Fiction. 3. Summer resorts—Fiction]
I. Bulloch, Bruce, ill. II. Title.
PZ7.D7593He 1985 [Fic] 84-19939
ISBN 0-89191-964-3

CAUTION!

This is not a normal book! If you read it straight through, it won't make sense.

Instead, you must start on page 1 and then turn to the pages where your choices lead you. Your first choice is ordinary enough: Should you take a day off from working at your family's resort or answer your mother when she calls to you (and probably not get the day off)? But after that, the choices may lead to new places, new people, exciting adventures, dangerous situations—or even an undersea world!

If you want to read this book, you must choose to

Turn to page 1.

RESORT

You can feel the sun shining brightly through the windows even before you open your eyes. But you just lie there. You don't want to get up to face another day of hard work.

When your dad and mom announced they were buying a resort, you thought life would be one long vacation. But it hasn't turned out that way. What good is it to live on a bay surrounded by woods and mountains if you hardly ever have time to enjoy it?

Finally you get up and get dressed. You've decided you deserve a change, and you're looking for adventure.

You write a note: "I'm taking a day's vacation. Don't worry, Mom. I'll be back for dinner."

You take three dollars from your money box. Then you tiptoe downstairs to the kitchen, grab four cookies and a banana, and slip out the back door.

As you run across the field, you hear your mother call.

Choices: **You pretend you don't hear (turn to page 2).**

You go back to see what she wants (turn to page 7).

You run to the road.

You feel guilty about not answering your mom, but you remind yourself that a day's vacation isn't asking much. Yesterday you pulled weeds and swept the lodge and worked in the little store and snack bar all afternoon.

Maybe if you had explained to Mom how much you needed a day off, she would have given it to you. But you were afraid you'd hear another lecture on how you all have to work if the resort is going to make a living for the family.

You walk along the road munching breakfast. You're going to town to look for some of the kids from school. You don't have any close friends yet because you only moved here two weeks before school let out. But you might see someone you know.

A pickup truck stops behind you, and the driver hollers, "Hey, kid, need a ride?"

Choices: You say, "Sure" (turn to page 3).
You refuse (turn to page 10).

You see two men in the cab of the truck. The bald guy gets out. "Sit in the middle, kid," he says.

"I'm only going to town," you say.

"That's where we're going," calls the red-haired driver.

You get in the cab in spite of the uneasy fear in the pit of your stomach.

The driver sounds jolly, but the other guy acts tense—as if they're up to something.

"Looks like rain, Joe," says the driver.

"Yeah, Red, those clouds are really black," agrees Joe.

When you get to town, you say, "I'll get off here."

"You ain't going nowhere," barks Joe.

Red adds, "We figure as long as we gave you a ride, you can help with a little project."

You gulp, "What do you want me to do?"

"You'll see. It's not a hard job, but you can do it a lot easier than either of us." Red speeds through town and out to the country.

You don't have any choice. You're sandwiched between two big guys.

Turn to the next page.

Finally the truck stops by a shed in a gravel pit. The guys get out, and you follow. It feels good to breathe fresh air again. The truck smelled of sweat and cigarette smoke.

Red gives the orders. "We need a little dynamite, kid. You're slim enough to climb through the window and hand it to us." Red takes a hammer and breaks the glass window.

Dynamite! That's dangerous stuff.

Choices: **You try to escape (turn to page 12).**
You see no way to escape (turn to page 46).

You take two loaves of freshly baked bread and the tomatoes that Mom put in a sack. You walk down to the boat shed and pick up two oars.

Dad is painting one of the boats on the dock.

"Going to Granny's island," you explain. You wonder why everyone calls her Granny, although she doesn't seem to be anyone's grandmother.

"Don't stay too long. Looks like a storm coming."

You look at the black clouds and choppy water. "I'll try to come back right away, but it's hard to get away from Granny."

"Maybe you should wait until tomorrow," suggests Dad.

Choices: You decide to wait even if it means cleaning that cabin (turn to page 16).
You decide to go. Granny needs her food, and you like to row when the waves bounce you around (turn to page 6).

You go down the ramp to the float which rises and falls with the tides. You push a boat into the water. Then you climb in, put the oars in the oarlocks, and start rowing. The boat rocks and slaps against the waves. You have to row hard to keep on course against the wind.

Then you notice a yellow boat from Sand's resort in the main channel. A girl with long black hair is standing in the boat and waving her arms as if she's trying to signal. You know that the tide is going out, causing strong currents in the channel. She must be in trouble.

Choices: **You go to help her (turn to page 8).**
You ignore her frantic signals (turn to page 11).
You row back home (turn to page 14).

Your mom says, "I need some help this morning. We have new people coming into Cabin 8, and it needs to be cleaned."

"Aw, Mom, I hate to clean cabins."

"Remember what your dad says, 'We're all working together to make this resort pay.' Someday we'll be able to hire help, but for now, we all have to pitch in."

"I'll do anything but clean cabins," you groan.

"Would you rather row out to Granny Morton's and deliver some bread and tomatoes?"

You groan again. "You know how she talks on and on. I never know how to get away from her."

"She's lonely, and she needs our help."

Choices: You decide to clean the cabin (turn to page 16).

You decide to visit Granny Morton (turn to page 5).

You've been warned not to go out in the channel when the tide is going out, but you can't let that poor girl be swept out to sea. You row with all your strength toward her boat.

You feel the pull of the tide now, and rowing is easier. The hard part will be getting back. Prickles of fear run up and down your spine.

Finally you reach her boat, and you grab hold of it. The girl looks too small to handle the boat alone.

"Quick, get in my boat," you order.

"Can we tie my boat to yours?"

"Forget your boat. We'll have enough trouble getting one boat back to land. Hurry!"

"I can't leave the boat. Dad rented it from the resort."

"There isn't time to argue. Get in my boat *now.*"

She gets in. You begin rowing back. You can't tell if you're making progress. You're afraid you'll never get home. The waves toss the boat about, and the current is strong. The little girl looks at you with confidence. "Thanks for rescuing me. I was awfully scared."

"We're not home yet." You have blisters on your palms from gripping the oars so tightly. Every stroke is harder than the last one. The waves splash in your boat.

Turn to page 125.

You say, "No, thanks, mister. I'm not going far."

He says, "No sense walking when you could be riding. Come on, I'll give you a doughnut."

"I don't want to ride." You don't like the way the guy's looking at you. Your folks always said never get in a stranger's car. You start running across the field.

The guys in the truck drive away.

You double back to the road and head for town.

As you reach the outskirts of town, you come to a street with sidewalks. As you pass a two-story house, a girl calls, "Hello."

You stop as you see Gloria Semper standing in the yard. She was in your homeroom at school.

"Come on over, I want to show you something," she calls.

You think Gloria is rather snobbish, so you hesitate.

Choices: You go into her yard (turn to page 18).
You keep on walking to town (turn to page 37).

You think, I'm not going out in that channel. With this wind it'll be doubly hard to row against the current.

You head for Granny's island. But you can't forget the little girl waving her arms. What if she drowns? You can't see her anymore, and you hope someone else helps her. You try to put her out of your mind.

Granny lives in a small gray cabin surrounded on three sides by evergreen trees.

You tie your boat to a driftwood log on shore, walk across the rocky beach, and follow the path to the cabin. When you knock on the door, Granny opens it.

"Land sakes, I sure am glad to see you. The batteries in my radio went dead, and I can't hear my radio preachers. I feel like my connection to heaven is broken. Oh, I know God is watching over me, but I feel better when I can hear the preachers telling me the good news. When you get to my age, you know you're soon going to leave this planet with its troubles and go to be with Jesus."

You finally get in a word. "I'll go to town and buy you new batteries."

Turn to page 15.

While both guys are looking at the window, you run, your legs churning as fast as they'll go.

You hear Joe yell, "Come back, you little creep, or you'll wish you had."

You glance back and see that Red is running after you. He's gaining! You try to run faster, but your lungs can't seem to get enough air.

Straight ahead of you is a large pond. On either side are steep cliffs.

Choices: **You run into the pond (turn to page 21).**

You head for the cliff to the right (turn to page 38).

You ask, "Where's your mom?"

"She works. I have to take care of my brothers this summer so she doesn't have to pay a baby-sitter."

You say, "I can stay a few minutes."

"Thanks a lot. I'll do something great for you someday." She rushes out of the yard like a sprinter in a hundred-yard dash. You have an uneasy feeling that you were conned into this assignment by a lot of phony flattery.

"Cookie," shouts Robby.

"Cookie," echoes Bobby.

You go to the kitchen. There are chocolate chip cookies in a jar. You give each twin a cookie, and you take two.

"Milk," says Robby.

"Milk," echoes Bobby.

You pour three glasses of milk. As you're drinking yours, you hear a crash. Robby dropped his glass.

Bobby cries, "I spill," and you see milk dribbling down his shirt. You grab Bobby's glass before he smashes it.

"Go to the living room," you order. You grab a bunch of paper towels. As you're picking pieces of glass from the sea of milk, you hear a loud crash. You rush into the living room and see a floor lamp lying on the rug.

Turn to page 31.

You row home as fast as you can. You run to the lodge and call the Sand's resort to tell the manager you saw a girl signaling for help from one of his rowboats.

He thanks you and says he'll try to rescue the girl with his powerboat.

You've had enough rowing for one stormy day, and you tell your mother you'll row to Granny's tomorrow. Mother asks you to mind the store while she sorts laundry.

This isn't a bad job because you can read a science fiction book when you're not busy. . . .

The hero is crawling through a rock tunnel on the planet Sleena hoping to escape from the hideous Ickmons. He hears someone coming.

You jump a foot as a shrill voice shouts in your ear, "I WANT A LOAF OF BREAD. How loud do you have to holler to get waited on?"

"I'm sorry. I didn't hear you come in." You hand the plump woman her bread and make change for the bill she hands you.

She leaves, and you pick up your book. . . .

Your hero is now trapped between two ferocious Ickmons.

"Ma, can we get double-dip cones?" Oh, no, here comes a family with six kids wanting ice-cream cones.

THE END

She hands you a paper. "I wrote down the kind I need. I usually keep an extra set, but I guess I used them. I prayed this morning that the Lord would send someone here so I could get new batteries. You're an answer to prayer."

You say, "I'll leave right away and get the batteries for you."

Granny says, "Sit down and have some cookies first." You hesitate for Granny bakes delicious cookies, but you want to get home before the storm gets worse.

Choices: You sit down (turn to page 126).
You say you must leave (turn to page 54).

The cabin is a mess. Ick. You scrub the sink, the counter, and the table. The last guests must have had small kids because there's sticky jam and syrup everywhere. You sweep cookie crumbs and sand from the floor. Then you get the mop and pail and scrub a patch of dried milk.

The bathroom is worse, and you douse it with disinfectant. As you sweep the closet, you notice a square brown object in the corner. You pick it up. It's a wallet that must have fallen from someone's pocket.

It has a twenty-dollar bill in it.

Choices: You take it back to the lodge (turn to page 66).

You keep the twenty dollars (turn to page 20).

Red grabs you and lifts you through the window. You carefully pick up a stick of dynamite and walk back to the window. "You guys get out of here, or I'll throw this at you! I'll blow you up and your truck, too."

Joe backs away.

Red says, "Hey, kid, we aren't going to hurt you. Come on, hand me that dynamite."

"The only way you're going to get it is right in the face. Now get going." You try to sound tough, but your forehead is dripping sweat, and the hand holding the dynamite is shaking.

Joe yells, "We'll give you a hundred dollars for helping us. That's good pay for a few minutes' work."

"No," you answer. "Get out of here before I throw this."

Joe jumps in the truck and starts the motor. "Come on, Red, before that stupid little nut blows us all up."

Red runs to the truck, and they drive away. You put down the dynamite. You write the truck's license number on a scrap of paper you find in the shed.

You put one leg out of the window very carefully. Shaking the shed might disturb the dynamite. As you're sitting on the sill with one leg in and one leg out, you hear an angry voice, "What are you doing in my shed?"

Turn to page 43.

You open the gate and walk over to Gloria. "What do you want to show me?"

"Come to the backyard."

You follow her to the fenced yard. A cute, little blond boy who's about two runs up to Gloria. "This is Robby," says Gloria, "and here's Bobby."

You blink and wonder if you're seeing double. The two boys look exactly alike. They're wearing green pants and yellow T-shirts. Their names are stamped on their shirts.

Robby comes to you. "Up," he says.

"That's amazing!" cries Gloria. "The twins are afraid of strangers, but they like you."

You pick up Robby, and he puts his chubby arms around your neck. Bobby holds out his arms. "Up, up," he demands. You put Robby down and pick up Bobby.

Gloria exclaims, "They love you. Children have a special sense to judge people. They know you're a really neat person."

You smile. Maybe Gloria is okay after all.

She adds, "Can you stay with the twins a few minutes while I run an errand? I won't be gone long."

Choices: You say no (turn to page 22).
You say yes (turn to page 13).

You go to see Judge Falkin, a friend of your father's. You explain what happened and why the Ospians are dangerous.

The judge believes you. He promises to call Washington, D.C., to alert officials to the danger.

The next morning, the judge calls to say a man's flying out from the Bureau of Sport Fisheries and Wildlife.

You object. "We need someone from the State Department. We're dealing with another nation. They can kill us."

"I did the best I could," answers the judge.

At four that afternoon, a man named Mr. Wingle arrives at the resort. He, your dad, and you walk to the float. You push the red button in the silver box to summon Zosta.

Mr. Wingle mutters, "I'm the new man in the office, so I get to talk to all the weirdos."

"I'm not crazy," you insist.

"I didn't say you were. But dreams sometimes seem real."

Mr. Wingle pulls a form from his pocket. "I have to bring a report back to the office. I'll put down that you were dreaming."

"I wasn't dreaming. It really happened. Zosta will come. You have to give her time."

Father looks stern. "You must face reality," he tells you. The men leave to go to Mr. Wingle's car.

Choices: You follow them (turn to page 90).
You wait for Zosta (turn to page 88).

You think, I deserve the money because the people didn't leave any tip. Most people leave something for the person who cleans up after them. And this cabin was one of the dirtiest I've ever cleaned. You put the twenty dollars in your pocket.

You throw the wallet in the garbage. It didn't have much else in it. Just a couple of pictures and a ticket stub.

But you feel uncomfortable. You wish you didn't have such a sensitive conscience. You concentrate on what you are going to buy with the money, but the guilty feeling won't go away.

Then Mother calls, "Uncle Max is here. Come and say hello."

You wrinkle your nose. Uncle Max is a physical fitness freak who always wants you to feel his muscles. He says you should get more exercise.

Uncle Max calls, "Want to go on an overnight hike in the mountains? Your mom says you've been working hard, and you deserve a treat."

Choices: You say you'll go, even though Uncle Max will probably wear you out (turn to page 25).

You decline, saying you have other plans (turn to page 41).

The pond is deeper than you expected. You swim toward the center. Red reaches the shore. You tread water in the middle of the pond.

Red just stands there, glaring at you. Apparently he doesn't want to get wet. Or maybe he can't swim.

"Hey, kid, come out of there before I come in after you," he threatens.

You look around, trying to figure out how to get out of the pond. The bank ahead is solid rock and steep. There aren't any toeholds or handholds. You feel icy cold, and you wish Red would go away. But he stands ready to pounce on you if you come to shore.

Red yells, "Hey, Joe. Come here. I need help."

You take a deep breath. You're tired of treading water. You try to float on your back, but your wet clothes pull you down.

Joe runs toward the pond.

Red hollers. "Hurry up, Joe. I need a swimmer to catch a big fish."

You shiver and swim closer to the rock bank. There's no way to get out of the pond except at the shallow end where Joe and Red are talking.

Turn to page 28.

Warning bells go off in your head. All this flattery is just part of the web Gloria is spinning to get you to take over her job for a while.

"I can't help you, Gloria. I'm in a big hurry." You put down the twin you're holding and head for the gate.

"Please, help me. It's terribly important," she pleads.

"Sorry, I'm too busy." You slip out the gate and hurry back to the sidewalk.

This is your day to goof off, and you aren't going to let someone trick you into taking care of twins.

But then you wonder if you made a mistake in refusing to help Gloria. Maybe you would have made a friend. It takes awhile to get acquainted in a new school, so you should try to be friendly to everyone.

You keep walking until you reach the business district. You try to think of something exciting to do.

Choices: You walk on the left side of the street (turn to page 37).
You walk on the right side of the street (turn to page 50).

You take the twins to their room so Gloria can clean up their messes without worrying about what they're doing next. You build block towers as fast as you can. They like to knock them down with their trucks.

Gloria comes in and says lunch is ready. She fixed tuna fish sandwiches. You eat in the kitchen, using plastic plates and cups. Both twins spill their milk, but nothing gets broken.

Gloria says, "This has been a hectic day. Sally and I are having a surprise birthday party for Tim Lander. He's the youth leader at our church and a really neat guy. The party's at her house, but I'm bringing the cake. I ordered it from the bakery, and I have to pick it up. Can you watch the twins while I run to town and get the cake?"

"Forget it," you answer. You're not going to stay alone with the twins again.

Then Gloria says brightly, "Why don't we both go? You push the stroller while I carry the cake."

Choices: You say, "Sure" **(turn to page 42).**
You say, "No way," and walk to town alone **(turn to page 50).**

You stuff your backpack with essentials and add an extra sweater, two science fiction books, a chocolate bar, and a sack of peanuts.

Uncle Max says he has plenty of dehydrated food. "I'll make my famous liver and spinach burgers for supper tonight."

"Sounds gross."

He says, "After you've hiked eight miles, you'll be ready to eat anything." He laughs loudly.

You climb in Uncle Max's car, and he drives to the mountains. At the end of the road, you leave the car and start hiking.

The first mile through the forest is level, but then the trail heads up with many switchbacks. Your pack feels heavy, and the straps bite into your shoulders. Your boots hurt your feet.

"Hey, let's stop," you pant.

"Not yet. That'll break our rhythm."

"I'm tired."

"A young person like you shouldn't feel tired. You ought to be out running three miles a day. Then you could run up this mountain without any effort."

"I don't like to run."

Turn to page 26.

"Try it for a while. The greatest thing in the world is to be healthy. We need to get our blood circulating. Come on, let's pick up our pace. Breathe deeply. Feel the oxygen going through your system."

You sit on a log and say, "Go on without me. I'm going to rest."

Uncle Max stops. "You can't be that tired. There's beautiful scenery ahead. You'll love it."

Uncle Max irritates you. He's a big bore, always preaching about health. And he won't even let you rest when you want to.

Choices: You decide to go back to the car and wait for Uncle Max (turn to page 118).
You go on with Uncle Max (turn to page 34).

Joe says, "I'm not getting my clothes wet for that stupid kid."

"But we need the kid!"

"Got a better idea. I'm going to use my ax to chop the lock out of the door," says Joe.

"But what if that dynamite isn't stable? You'll shake it too much."

"I'll be real careful," promises Joe.

The two men walk back to the shed.

You swim to the shallow end of the pond and walk out. The wind is blowing, and it chills your wet body. You run to the road, trying to get your frozen blood to circulate.

A little later you hear a loud explosion. The dynamite shed! You turn and see flashes of light and hear more explosions.

Choices: **You run back to see what's happened (turn to page 92).**

You keep walking toward home (turn to page 129).

You fall asleep on the grass as you wait.

The next thing you know, Mom is hugging you. "Are you all right?" she cries.

You open your eyes and sit up. "I'm okay. Why is the lodge locked?"

Dad says, "We were at church arranging a memorial service for you. We thought you were dead. The Coast Guard has been looking for your boat or your body. You vanished without a trace."

Mom sits beside you. Tears glisten in her eyes. "I never gave up hope, but where have you been?"

You tell them about the bubble and the Ospians.

Dad says, "Sounds as if you had a strange dream. You must have passed out in your boat. Maybe you hit your head on the side when a wave hit."

"But, Dad, I saw the Ospians, and they want to stop people from polluting their water."

"With all the science fiction you read, it's no wonder you have strange dreams," Mom says. "You go lie down, and I'll fix you some food."

Choices: **You decide to forget about the Ospians. It must have been a dream (turn to page 44).**

You know it's up to you to save the world from the Ospians (turn to page 36).

You want to look around the city. "Now that everything turned out all right, I'm going to do some sight-seeing," you tell Gloria.

She scowls. "You're not going to leave me alone with the boys, are you?"

"You can handle them."

"What about my cake? How will I get my cake home?"

"You must know somebody who can help you. I took a day off from the resort to have fun, but I haven't had any fun at all. I would have been better off working at home than helping you take care of these monsters."

"They're not monsters."

"They do need civilizing. See you around, Gloria."

You get off the ferry and wonder what you should do.

Choices: You decide to walk along the waterfront (turn to page 64).
You walk across the overpass to First Avenue (turn to page 73).
You walk to the public market (turn to page 115).

The little terrors have disappeared. You look in all the downstairs rooms; then you head upstairs. You find them in their parents' bedroom. They've smeared the ivory walls with red lipstick and blue eye shadow.

"Pretty," says Robby.

"Not pretty. Go outside," you command.

The telephone rings. Gloria says sweetly, "Can you stay a little longer? It's taking longer than I planned."

You sputter, "Listen, Gloria, you better get home while your house is still standing! I can't watch the twins and clean up their messes at the same time."

"What kind of messes?"

"Milk and broken glass. Smashed lamps. Makeup on the walls. Come quick!"

"I'll be right there."

Gloria comes back fuming. "You sure didn't watch them."

"I never took care of two-year-old twins before. I didn't know you couldn't let them out of your sight."

"Mom's going to skin me alive when she sees the lamp and the wall."

You tell her, "Next time you con someone into taking care of your brothers, warn them what to expect."

Choices: You storm out of the house (turn to page 61).

You stay to help Gloria (turn to page 24).

You wake up in a large, transparent bowl—lying on a sponge mattress. You wonder if you're in heaven.

Dark water surrounds the bowl. Big eyes are watching you. You shiver in fear for these are the strangest creatures you've ever seen. The faces have no noses, and the heads have no hair. Their skin is silver-gray, and their arms and legs end in flippers. One creature points a flipper at you. Now more large, staring eyes appear.

You feel as if you're in a goldfish bowl. But where are you, and how did you get here?

A voice booms, "I see you finally regained consciousness. We saved your life by replacing the water in your lungs with oxygen."

"Thank you, but who are you?" you say. You look up and see a face looking down at you. It's like a fish face with gill-like cheeks and a large mouth that moves as it speaks.

The creature says, "I am Zosta from the country of Osp located in what you call the Pacific Ocean. I have been sent to make contact with you land creatures. We've set up a temporary settlement close to shore."

Turn to page 39.

You trudge on, trying to keep up with Uncle Max. You pass a green lake surrounded by evergreen trees, but as you go higher, the trees thin out. You see alpine meadows with wild flowers and snow-covered peaks. God did a fantastic job when he landscaped this area.

But then the dark clouds above you begin to drop rain, and the clouds obscure the mountains.

"It's just a shower," says Uncle Max.

You reach the top of the ridge and start down toward a small lake.

"That's Sapphire Lake, where we're going to camp," says Uncle Max.

You say, "That didn't seem like eight miles—more like eighty."

Uncle Max laughs loudly.

When you reach the lake, you take your pack off. You feel light enough to float away. "I like hiking, because it feels so good to stop," you tell Uncle Max.

The rain finally stops, and Max builds a fire and starts cooking liver and spinach burgers.

You eat them because you're so hungry.

Turn to next page.

As it gets dark, you crawl into your sleeping bag in the pup tent. You put on mosquito repellent to discourage the insects that think you came for their nourishment. You soon fall asleep, but you wake up as you hear groaning.

"What's wrong?" you cry.

Uncle Max moans, "I think it's my appendix. Oh, it hurts."

"What can I do?"

"Nothing—until it gets light. Then maybe you can go for help."

Finally morning comes. You whisper, "Uncle Max, you awake?"

"Can't sleep with my insides on fire."

"I'm going to find help."

"Hurry, please."

You grab a banana and some raisins and start hiking up to the ridge. You try to remember where you came up. You see footprints on a snowfield. You trudge across the crunchy snow, but when you get to the other side you can't find the trail.

Choices: You keep walking down the mountain (turn to page 40).

You climb back to the ridge to look for the trail (turn to page 74).

After resting awhile, you tell your mother you're biking to town.

Mom says, "You should stay home and rest."

"I feel fine, Mom. I need some fresh air and exercise."

"But you had such a terrible experience." She feels your forehead to check for a fever.

"Mom, there's nothing wrong with me now." You finally convince her you're okay, and you bike to town. You have to find someone who will believe your story about the Ospians.

Turn to page 19.

You walk past the bakery and breathe in the enticing smell. Then you see some kids you met at school, and you cross the street to talk to them. It's Brad, Nora, Chris, and a couple of younger kids you don't know.

Brad says, "Hey, want to go to a puppet show?"

"Sounds great." You figure it will be more exciting than walking along the street.

Brad asks, "You got fifty cents?"

"Sure. Where's the show?" you ask.

"At the high school auditorium. It's a troupe from Europe. They're really funny," explains Chris.

"It starts at one. We've got plenty of time," adds Nora.

You walk along with the kids as they head toward the high school. It's fun to be with friends.

"Here's the plan," says Brad. "The tickets cost three dollars, but we'll each put in fifty cents to buy one ticket for me. Then I'll go to the fire exit in the hall and let you guys in."

You gulp. You don't like the plan, but you want to make friends.

Choices: You give Brad fifty cents (turn to page 72).

You change your mind (turn to page 51).

You scramble up the steep, rocky hill, grabbing hold of scrubby trees growing in the cracks. One of the trees comes up by the roots, and you fall backwards. You land in a heap at the bottom of the hill. A big hand jerks you up by your right arm. Red's features are contorted in an ugly frown.

"If you don't do what we say, you aren't going to live to tell about it," he snarls.

He drags you back toward the shed.

Joe reaches in and unfastens the window catch. He pushes the broken window open. You don't want to help them steal dynamite, but what can you do? Those guys are much bigger than you, and there are two of them.

You can see the dynamite stacked on shelves on the wall opposite the window. Prickles of fear run up your spine. Your hands are shaking. What if you drop a stick? You might be blown to bits.

Red points at the window. "Hurry up, kid."

Choices: You move toward the window (turn to page 46).

You refuse (turn to page 17).

You ask, "How do you know English?"

"We pick up your radio and TV signals. It was not difficult to learn your language."

"How can I get out of here?"

"First I'll tell you what I want you to do. We need someone who can speak to your leaders for us. You must tell them to stop polluting the water!"

Choices: You say, "I can't do that. I'm just a kid" **(turn to page 108).**

You agree to try **(turn to page 47).**

There are more trees now, and you soon come to the forest. You see what you think is a trail, and you follow it, but then it stops. Panic sweeps over you. You can't get lost, not with Uncle Max sick and depending on you to get help.

You keep walking, but with all the big trees, you haven't any idea whether you're going in the right direction or not.

You call, "Help, help," hoping there are other hikers around, but no one answers. You hear a crashing noise in the brush. A large brown bear is heading for you.

You run, jumping over logs and scampering around trees. You glance back. The bear is still coming. You leap over a patch of nettles, but as you come down, your left foot lands in an animal hole, and you go sprawling on the ground. Before you can get up, the bear reaches you. You can smell his fishy breath. Man, does he need a breath mint. He sniffs you, while you brace yourself for his first bite. You hide your face in the dust and fir needles and wait. Your heart is pounding at a furious rate.

Turn to page 96.

Uncle Max leaves, and you head for the door of the lodge. Before you can go out, a man storms in the door and shouts at your mother, "Have you cleaned Cabin 8 yet?"

"It's clean," answers Mom. "Did you forget something?"

"My daughter left her wallet. Do you have it?"

Mom turns to you. "Did you find a wallet when you cleaned Cabin 8?"

Your face feels hot and your hands sweat. "Ah—yeah—I'll go get it," you stammer.

You run to Cabin 8 and pull the lid off the garbage can. But Dad's already emptied it in the dumpster. You'll never find the wallet now. You pull the twenty dollars from your pocket and run back to the lodge.

The whole family is waiting for you. The younger kids run around swatting one another while their mother yells at them.

You hand the twenty-dollar bill to the man. "Here's the money. I guess the wallet got thrown away."

A teenage girl screams. "My picture! My picture of Alex! What do you mean it's been thrown out?"

Everyone, including Mom, is looking at you suspiciously as you try to think of a story to explain this.

Turn to page 120.

You figure the twins can't get into mischief while they're riding in a stroller. The twins are happy about going out. Gloria puts red jackets with hoods on them.

You walk along the sidewalk with Gloria pushing the double stroller. You wish she'd invite you to the party, but she doesn't say anything.

As you come to the bakery, Gloria says, "You watch the twins while I get the cake."

You breathe in the delicious, sweet air as you feel hunger pangs starting though you just had lunch.

The kids have the same reaction.

"Cookie," screams Robby.

"Cookie," hollers Bobby.

Gloria buys them each a large sugar cookie with a raisin face. They sit happily munching their cookies.

The bakery lady has to go in the back to find Gloria's cake. You stand looking at the cinnamon rolls, wondering if you should buy some. These have lots of raisins—just the way you like them.

Gloria shrieks, "The twins! Where are the twins?" You look at the empty stroller with a sinking feeling.

Turn to page 45.

A large man comes racing across the gravel pit, his face red with rage. "You little thief . . ."

"Hey, let me explain," you cry.

"You'll tell your story to the sheriff," he barks.

"I don't want your dynamite. I was kidnapped because some guys thought I was small enough to fit in the window."

"Where are your pals now?"

"They're not my pals. They left when I threatened to throw dynamite at them."

"Get down from the windowsill."

As you slip to the ground, the man clamps a big hand on your upper right arm. "Come with me while I call the sheriff."

You're scared. What if the sheriff doesn't believe your story? What if he thinks you were trying to steal the dynamite?

When you get to the man's house, he calls the sheriff on the phone in the kitchen.

Choices: You watch for a chance to run away (turn to page 86).

You wait to tell your story to the sheriff (turn to page 48).

Mother brings you chicken soup and fruit salad in bed. Maybe someday you'll write a fantasy story about the Ospians. They seemed so real at the time. But you're not going to talk about them anymore. You don't want people to think you're weird.

You look at the tiny silver-colored box. You can't remember where you got it, but you collect a lot of odd stuff. Somehow this piece of junk worked its way into your pocket and dream.

THE END

"They can't have gone far," you say as you rush out the door and look up and down the street. You can't see any little red jackets.

"You go this way; I'll go that way." Gloria starts running toward the middle of town. You go the other way, but you stop as you hear Gloria scream, "Look."

You run to Gloria. She's pointing to the ferry. Two small red-jacketed figures stand by the railing of the upper deck.

"It can't be them. How could they have gotten there so fast?" you say.

Gloria runs toward the ferry dock.

Choices: **You follow her** **(turn to page 69)****.**
You keep looking around town **(turn to page 117)****.**

You climb through the window. You pick up a stick of dynamite and carefully hand it to Red. You hand the next stick to Joe. They load them in the back of their truck in wooden boxes. You keep handing them sticks, wishing the whole nightmare was over. You wish you had stayed home and worked at the resort.

You decide you're not going to get back in that truck—not when it's loaded with dynamite.

Finally Red says, "Okay, kid, this is the last stick." He puts it in the truck and then comes back to help you out of the shed. "We'll give you a lift to town."

You shake your head. "I'll walk from here. I don't want to ride with all that dynamite."

"Don't be silly." He grabs you by the shoulder. "We want you to come with us. Understand?"

You try to pull away, but he grabs your arm in a viselike grip and pulls you over to the truck. Again you're sandwiched between the two big guys, and you feel sick to your stomach. Maybe they aren't going to let you go. Maybe they're afraid you'll squeal on them, and that's exactly what you intend to do.

Red drives away from the pit, but he doesn't take the road toward town. Instead he heads for the mountains.

Turn to page 62.

You say, "I'll try, but people may not believe me because I'm a kid."

"You must make them believe you, for your people are in great danger," warns Zosta.

You shiver. "What do you mean?"

"Our high commander in Osp wants to melt the ice at both poles and flood the land."

"How will you do that?"

"We have the technology to move hot magma from within the earth to the poles. But I convinced our commander to let me talk to your leaders. We can live peacefully with land people if you will stop polluting our water with oil, chemicals, and garbage."

You cry, "How can I convince people I'm telling the truth?"

"If you get one of your leaders to come to the shore, I'll swim up and talk to him. Take the silver box on your right. You push the red button to summon me."

You pick up the box which is smaller than a candy bar. "Can you breathe air?" you ask.

"Only for short times, but I can live longer in air than you can live in water. Now I will activate your bubble so it will rise to the surface. Remember your mission and save the people of earth lands."

Turn to page 52.

You sit by the table in a big kitchen. The man sits by the phone near the back window. As you wait for the sheriff, the man's son comes home. He's Tony—a kid from school.

His dad tells him he caught you trying to steal his dynamite.

"What were you trying to do—get stuff to blow up the school?" asks Tony.

You tell the story of being kidnapped, but Tony only laughs. What if he tells everyone at school you're a thief? No one will want to be your friend.

You plead, "Tony, you gotta believe me. I'd never mess around with dynamite. I'm scared of the stuff."

Tony sits beside you. "Tell me who you're working for."

"I'm not working for anyone." You keep talking, trying to convince Tony you're telling the truth.

Tony whispers, "I can help you escape. How much you got?"

"Three dollars."

"Very funny. I gotta have more than that. The sheriff is a friend of Dad's. He'll take Dad's word against yours and lock you up."

You swallow.

Choices: You offer Tony a bribe (turn to page 53).

You refuse Tony's help (turn to page 113).

You try crashing into the door with your other shoulder. Now you have two sore shoulders.

You yank up the old braided rug on the floor to cushion your right shoulder for another try at breaking the door.

You stare down at the trapdoor you've uncovered. With effort, you pull the heavy door open and look down at the darkness. Maybe you'll find another door down there.

You climb down a rickety ladder and step on the dirt floor. In the dim light you see shelves on the walls. A few canning jars of food stand on them. You're hungry, but as your eyes get used to the dim light, you see that the food in the jars is moldy. The cellar smells rotten, as if a dead rat might be decaying in one of the dark corners.

No doors lead to the outside. Shivers run up and down your spine. You've got to get out of this creepy cell.

You grab the ladder. It crashes down on top of you, knocking you over. You untangle yourself from the broken ladder. You're stuck in this smelly, dark dungeon with no way to get out!

THE END

You stop to watch a bearded fellow who has set up an easel under the drugstore awning. He's painting a picture. He's splashing horizontal stripes of blue, green, and black paint on a large rectangular canvas. He has several finished paintings standing against the building.

You look at the prices. Two hundred dollars for jiggly lines of different colors! You feel excited. You could paint stuff like that.

The fellow turns to you. "Want to buy a painting?" he asks in a teasing voice.

"Not me. Hey, do you sell many paintings?"

"Quite a few. Sold one yesterday for three hundred dollars."

You run to the art supply store and spend your money on paint and paper. You hurry home to start your new career. Only one thing worries you. Will people buy your stuff if they know you're only a kid?

THE END

"I changed my mind. I'm not going," you tell Brad.

He answers, "What's the matter? You chicken?"

"No, but I don't like this kind of action. Not my style." You leave.

But you keep thinking about the puppet show. It would be fun to see. You only have three dollars, so if you buy a ticket, you won't have money for lunch.

You feel hungry as you start to think about it. You go in the supermarket. Sometimes somebody is giving out free samples. You pick up a bite of doughnut in the bakeshop and a tiny paper cup of clam chowder from a lady who says, "Be sure to tell your mother to buy Seaside Chowder."

You're still hungry, but you go to the high school and buy a ticket for the puppet show. You don't see the kids who were going to get in on one ticket. Apparently their scheme didn't work.

The puppets are almost life size, and they can dance, pick up balls, and ride bicycles. You wonder how the puppet masters learn to control the strings without getting them tangled. You're glad you don't have strings on you.

THE END

The bubble rises and floats on the water's surface. A door on top flips open, and a rope ladder descends. You climb to the top. As you're wondering if you can swim to shore, your boat appears, pushed by two Ospians.

You holler, "Thank you," as they disappear in the water.

You climb in and row home. The boat has two oars—the Ospians must have found your missing oar.

You don't know how long you've been gone. You pull your boat up on the float and hurry to the lodge. But a sign on the door says, LODGE AND STORE CLOSED. Everything is locked, and you don't have your key. It's strange that both Dad and Mom have left.

Choices: You sit on the lawn to wait for your parents (turn to page 29).

You bike to town (turn to page 19).

"I've got forty dollars in my money box at home. I'll give you that," you promise.

"Forty dollars. Not bad."

"I've been saving for a new bike."

"A ten speed won't do you any good in jail. I'll be over to collect the money later today."

"How do I get away?"

"I'll distract Dad, and you run out the front door." Tony walks over to his dad. He points to the back window. "Look, Dad, there's the deer that eats our apples."

"Where? I don't see it."

You don't wait to hear more. You run through the living room and out the front door. Your heart is pounding, but you keep running down the highway.

Tony yells, "Hey, you stop. STOP!" He runs after you, but he doesn't try to catch you. He's more interested in the forty dollars.

Then you hear the siren of the sheriff's car. You duck behind a bush until the car goes by. You cut across a pasture. You start thinking about Tony. He's a rat. He can make your life miserable by demanding more and more money to keep his mouth shut.

Choices: You decide to go to the sheriff and tell the truth (turn to page 91).

You'd like to refuse to pay Tony, but you're afraid (turn to page 106).

You run down to your boat. You untie it and jump in the bow as you push it into the water. You row as hard as you can against the strong wind. Between the rain and the splashing waves, you are soon soaked.

The waves get higher and wilder, and you have trouble keeping the bow pointed into the waves. You know if your boat takes them sideways, it might capsize.

You push your dripping hair from your eyes just as a big wave splashes your boat. You reach for the oar. It's gone! Yipe! The boat almost turns over. You try to control it with one oar, but it's no use. The waves are too big.

You scream, "HELP! HELP!" but the wind swallows your cry. A big wave overturns your boat. You fight the cold salt water, trying to find your way to the surface. You come up and gulp some air. You holler, "HELP! I'M DROWNING!"

A wave splashes over you. You're being pulled down in the icy water. You're swallowing water in a frantic effort to get air. Your last thought before you black out is that you're going to beat Granny to heaven.

Choices: This is THE END.
This just seems like THE END (turn to page 32).

"Gloria, let's ask the sheriff to hold the ferry and get the kids off."

You and Gloria run into the sheriff's office. Gloria exclaims, "My brothers are only two, and they're alone on the ferry." She looks out the window and sees the ferry pulling away from the dock. "Please, make the ferry come back."

"Can't do that, but I'll radio the captain and have somebody look for them," the sheriff's deputy says. "Description?"

"Red jackets with hoods. Underneath they're wearing T-shirts that say Robby and Bobby."

He nods. "That's enough description."

Turn to page 56.

The deputy radios to the ferry captain. A little later the captain calls back to say, "The boys are safe. A ferry worker is watching them. They're determined to get into mischief, but we're just as determined to keep them from harming themselves, anyone else, or our property."

Gloria goes to the bakery and picks up the cake. You push the empty stroller home for her. She says, "This gives me time to do a few things for the party. But I'll have to watch the clock and meet the ferry when it gets back. I hope the boys are all right."

"I'm sure they're okay, but I feel sorry for the ferry worker who got baby-sitting duty."

When you come to Gloria's house, you say, "See you around."

"Thanks for your help," she says. Then she adds, "If you're not doing anything, why don't you come to the party tonight?"

You grin. "Yeah, sure. I'll be there."

You turn a handspring on the grass. It's fun to have a new friend—actually three friends if you count the twin terrors.

THE END

Almost before you realize what you're doing, you take off after the thief. You're a fast runner, and you overtake him and grab the woman's purse.

He swings his fist at you, but you dodge his blow. You run as he hollers, "I'll sic my gang on you."

You glance over your shoulder. He's standing there glaring at you. You bring the purse back to the woman. She says, "Thank you. You're very brave."

"Glad I caught him."

"I just cashed my paycheck. I would have had a hard time without it. I'd like to give you a reward."

"Oh, no, I don't want a reward," you insist.

"At least let me take you through the aquarium. That's where I work."

You look up the street and see the thief talking to two tough-looking guys.

Choices: You say, "I gotta go now," and leave quickly (turn to page 137).

You go to the aquarium (turn to page 114).

You pull a dollar from your pocket and walk over to the couple. "May I buy a hot dog?"

The woman says, "Are you alone?"

"I got separated from my uncle. He has the food."

"Poor child," she exclaims. "Sit down." She takes the wiener from her stick, puts it in a bun, and hands it to you. You hold out the dollar, but she shakes her head. "Keep your money."

You bite into the hot dog, thinking you've never tasted anything so good. You've never been this hungry before.

The man gives you another hot dog. You devour it and stand up. "Thanks a lot. I have to find my uncle."

The woman hands you a paper bag. "Here's an apple and some cookies—in case you don't find your uncle right away."

"Super! That's sure nice of you," you say with a smile. You munch on cookies as you walk.

You keep thinking you'll meet Uncle Max coming down, but you don't see anyone. You come to a ridge, where a sign points to Sapphire Lake. You head in that direction.

Finally you see a blue lake in a valley below the ridge. You hurry to the lake, but there's no sign of your uncle.

You are tired and cold, and you crawl into your sleeping bag. What could have happened to Uncle Max?

Turn to page 116.

Gloria marches to the wheelhouse and faces a man with a red face. "Keep out of here! Can't you read the signs?" he explodes.

Gloria starts to cry. "My little brothers came to the wheelhouse, but now they're lost."

He growls, "Why don't you watch your kids? I had a perfect record before today."

Gloria's voice trembles, "At least you're alive. I'm afraid Robby and Bobby fell overboard!"

The captain sighs and speaks into a microphone. "Attention, everyone. Two small boys in red jackets are lost. If you see them, notify a crew member. Don't try to capture them alone."

You and Gloria again search the top deck and then the other decks, but there's no sign of the boys. Finally the ferry begins to move. Gloria mutters, "Nobody cares about my lost brothers."

You keep walking around, hoping you'll see some sign of the twins. You look out a window and see the tall buildings of the city. People hurry toward the stairways to go to their cars.

You say, "If the twins get off in the city, we'll never find them." You realize you've said the wrong thing, as Gloria begins crying again. Then you hear the sound of car horns.

Turn to page 81.

"Zosta, I'm sorry," you call, as she dives into the water.

You think, maybe it is a foreign plot to scare us. But then you remember your bubble and all the strange creatures looking at you. They couldn't have been costumed people.

Mr. Wingle made a wrong choice—a choice that may mean the end of land creatures.

THE END

You're sorry Gloria has a mess to clean up, but she should have known it wasn't safe to leave the twins with someone who didn't have any experience with little kids.

You're hungry. You pull out the money in your pocket. Three dollars. You wonder if you should buy lunch.

Choices: You go to town to find a restaurant (turn to page 75).
You go home for a free lunch (turn to page 134).

Red turns off on a logging road. He's driving slowly so he won't shake up the dynamite, but you think what a big explosion all that dynamite could make, and you shiver.

Finally Red stops and says, "End of the line."

Joe gets out of the truck, and you climb out, too. He clamps his big beefy hand on your shoulder and steers you toward a small cabin.

"Let me go." You squirm, but you can't get away from Joe.

He says, "We ain't going to hurt you, but it wouldn't be smart to let you loose until we can get away from here."

Choices: You go with Joe (turn to page 122).
You scream (turn to page 67).

You look longingly at the city, but you decide to stay and help Gloria with the twins.

You all go upstairs. You sit down on an upholstered bench. The twins sit still a whole minute. Then they're off and running. That nap in the car gave them a new spurt of energy.

You grab Robby, and Gloria grabs Bobby. You take them outside. They pull you and Gloria up the stairs and around the deck.

By the time the ferry docks, you're exhausted. You all go back to the bakery. Gloria carries her cake while you push the twins in their stroller.

When you get to the house, Gloria says, "Thanks a lot. Oh, I hope you'll come to the party tonight."

"Sounds great. I'll be there."

"My friend." Bobby pats your leg.

"Bobby learned a new word," exclaims Gloria.

You pick up Bobby. Robby pulls on your hand. "Friend, friend," he chants.

"They just love you," purrs Gloria. "Will you play with them while I run to Sally's?"

She rushes off as you yell, "Wait a minute."

THE END

You walk along the waterfront street. Tourists crowd around a seafood stand. A teenager bounces along to the rhythm of his radio music. A bum shuffles by with his head down looking for some lost change.

You see a young woman steering her motorized wheelchair along the sidewalk. Suddenly a tall kid runs up to her and grabs her brown purse. She screams.

Choices: You run after the robber (turn to page 57).

You don't do anything (turn to page 100).

You hand the wallet to your mother. She sighs. "I'll mail it to the family who stayed in that cabin. I wish people would remember to take all their belongings with them."

The next week your mother gets a letter from a girl named Karen. She shows it to you.

"Dear Mrs. Mason,

"Thank you for sending my wallet. I didn't think I'd ever see it again. I worked hard picking strawberries to earn that money. I'm planning to buy a doll for a refugee girl who never had a doll. Other people at our church are donating clothes and furniture for the Vietnamese family, but I think it's important for the little girl to have a doll."

You have a warm feeling. You had a part in helping, too.

THE END

You keep screaming as loud as you can, hoping there's a logger or hiker or someone who might hear you.

Red jumps out of the truck. "Make that kid shut up."

Joe tries to clamp a hand over your mouth, but you bite him. Joe hollers. You pull loose and race into the woods.

Red yells, "What'd you let the kid get away for?"

"I'm bleeding," Joe screams. "Wait'll I get my hands on . . ." He dashes toward the woods. You run as fast as you can, leaping over fallen logs, darting between bushes and trees. Then your jeans leg gets caught in a blackberry vine, and you fall in the thorny bush. Ouch! You can't get loose. You're sure to be caught.

You hear Red's voice. "Come back, Joe. We don't have time to play hide-and-seek with the brat. We got a big job to pull."

"Yeah, guess you're right." Joe hurries back to the truck.

Red guns the motor. You're relieved to see the last of those crooks and their dynamite, but you have no idea where you are. You pull yourself loose from the blackberry thorns and stand up. You wish you were home by the fireplace.

You start running along the road, back the way the truck came.

Turn to page 105.

Hours later you hear a man's voice. "Hello, down there. I'm coming after you. Don't move."

You look up to see a man climbing toward you on a rope held by several people on the ridge above. He ties a rope around you. "Lucky you didn't go over that cliff. Any broken bones?"

"My left arm hurts the worst."

He examines you and puts a splint on your arm. Some other people come down with a rope stretcher. You're amazed at the skillful way they maneuver on the steep incline. They put you on the stretcher and carry you to a meadow to wait for a helicopter.

Your rescuers are from the Mountain Rescue Council, and they've been looking for you.

You're taken to the hospital where a doctor puts a cast on your broken arm. As the doctor leaves, your mother and father rush into the room. Mother cries, "I've been so worried."

"I'm okay, Mom," you tell her. You look at your cast. You're going to miss rowing and swimming. But you won't miss cleaning cabins and grounds. No disaster is all black.

THE END

Gloria runs to the ferry dock with you close behind. The ticket taker stops her. "You have to have a ticket, miss."

She sputters, "I don't want to ride. I just want to get my brothers. They're only two years old. I have to get them off the ferry."

"Ferry's ready to leave," he says, as if nothing can change the schedule.

Choices: **You say, "We better buy tickets"** **(turn to page 97).**
You say, "Don't give him any money. I've got a better idea" **(turn to page 55).**

Zosta talks fast. She tells of the Ospian kingdom which has lived in peace for many centuries. She asks that they be guaranteed unpolluted water.

Mr. Wingle frowns. "I'll have to talk to my boss, and he'll have to talk to his boss."

Zosta snaps, "You must give me your promise soon or the ruler of Osp will order the polar ice caps melted. You have only a short time to save land creatures from a terrible flood."

Mr. Wingle clenches his fists. "I don't believe you can do that. Tell your leaders we are not afraid of threats. I recognize your accent. You're really from the Soviet Union. You're trying to scare us. Go back to your sub, and tell them it won't work." Mr. Wingle marches away.

Choices: You let him go (turn to page 60).
You run after him (turn to page 136).

Time goes slowly until one o'clock. You all stop at the bakery and buy cinnamon rolls. They're still warm and have lots of raisins.

Then you walk over to the high school. Nora leads the way to the back of the school where there's a fire exit near the auditorium. The door only opens from the inside.

You wait. Your stomach feels funny. You're afraid you're going to get in trouble. Even if no one catches you, you don't think you'll enjoy the show. But you don't want your new friends to think you're a coward.

Choices: You leave and go home (turn to page 138).

You stay (turn to page 89).

You walk along First Avenue. It's not the best part of town. A drunk staggers down the street and stops right in front of you. "Say there, want to earn ten dollars?"

"Doing what?"

"Just a little investment. You give me a dollar, and I'll give you back ten."

A kid walks by and advises you, "Don't let him con you out of any money."

"Keep away from me, Norm. You're a snitch," complains the drunk.

"I don't have any money," you explain.

The drunk staggers on.

Norm asks, "You hungry?"

"Yeah, sort of."

"Come on. I'll show you where you can get free food." He leads the way to a mission. A woman is dishing up soup to a motley line of people.

Choices: You say, "Hey, I don't need charity." You leave (turn to page 135).

You take a bowl of soup (turn to page 133).

When you get back to the ridge, you follow it until you find a trail marker. Then you hike down the trail, crossing snowfields and finally coming to the forest.

You pass a green lake surrounded by trees. You see a family having a picnic. You call, "How far to the campground?"

"Only a couple of miles."

"Thanks." You try to hike faster even though your feet are sore and your stomach is growling for food. Poor Uncle Max needs help as fast as you can get it.

Turn to page 80.

You go into Mama's Pizza Kitchen and order a wedge of pizza and a Coke. You wonder how Gloria's getting along with her twin brothers. You're sure not going to take care of those monsters again. But you smile as you think about them.

You've heard people talk about the terrible twos. Your mom tells about you washing a window with a mashed banana and trying to cut a flower out of the living room drapes with blunt scissors. Guess it takes awhile to learn the rules of acceptable behavior.

Maybe you could stop by Gloria's once in a while so she could get a rest from the twins. You'd know better what to expect next time.

THE END

You go to the coffee shop and buy a doughnut. Over the loudspeaker, the captain tells everyone to watch for the lost twins. You relax. Someone'll find the boys. You're tired of looking.

Gloria storms up to you. "How can you think of eating at a time like this?"

"Somebody'll see them and report it. People remember your brothers."

She begins to cry. "Maybe no one's seen them. I'm so afraid they fell overboard. What'll I tell Mom and Dad? It's all my fault."

The ferry starts up again.

You say, "Come on, Gloria. There are lots of places we haven't looked yet. The twins are on this ship, and we're going to find them."

Later, as the ship gets close to the city, people head for their cars. You still haven't found the boys. You hear the sound of car horns.

Turn to page 81.

You look for a telephone. You go into a small restaurant and ask politely, "May I use your phone?"

"Pay phone's up that way." The man points to his left.

"But I don't have any money."

"Beat it, kid," he growls.

You leave. What if no one will let you call home?

Then you notice an older woman in a second-hand shop. She reminds you of Granny Morton. You go in. "Please, could I use your phone? I lost my ferry ticket, and I don't have any way to get home."

She asks, "Where do you live?"

"It's across the sound. I'm afraid it's a long-distance call, but I'll send you some money."

"Don't you worry about that. You call your family."

"Thank you very much." Your dad won't be happy to come to the city to get you. As you dial, you wonder how you'll explain why you're here.

THE END

You blink back the tears. There must be a way to escape. You need something sharp to cut the rope. You sit up and then stand up. You hop toward the kitchen corner and manage to pull a drawer open.

Ah, a paring knife. You maneuver to pick it up, and very carefully you cut the ropes on your hands. Unfortunately you also cut your hand. You grab a wrinkled tissue from your pocket to stop the bleeding. Cutting the rope from your ankles is a breeze now that your hands are free.

Looking around the room, you note that the windows are too small to crawl through. You'll have to figure out a way to open the door.

You run against the door several times, slamming it with your left shoulder. It doesn't collapse like doors on TV do. You just get a sore shoulder.

Choices: You keep trying muscle power (turn to page 49).

You stop and try brain power (turn to page 132).

"Yeah," Norm answers, "terrible things happen."

You wish you could help Norm. But you don't know how. So you say, "Want the rest of my soup?"

He nods, and you push your bowl to him. You write your address on a paper and hand it to him. "Why don't you write me and let me know how you're getting along. I'll pray for you."

He shakes his head. "I don't like to write."

"If you put down your address, I'll write to you."

"What are you? Some sort of missionary to street kids? I can take care of myself."

You run back to the ferry terminal. You're anxious to get back to the resort even if you have to work. You're glad you trust Jesus to guide your life. You pray that Norm will accept him as his Savior.

THE END

Finally you come to a campground. You find a park employee emptying garbage cans, and you tell him your uncle has appendicitis. He takes you to the ranger station in his truck.

The ranger calls for a helicopter, and you get to ride with the rescuers. You like looking down at the forests and lakes, but you're too worried about Uncle Max to really enjoy it.

The helicopter lands beside Sapphire Lake. The pilot and the medic run over to Uncle Max with a stretcher.

Uncle Max sits up, saying, "I can walk to the chopper."

But his face looks chalk white, and the men persuade him to lie on the stretcher.

They load Uncle Max in the helicopter, and you take off. You land in the hospital parking lot, and soon Uncle Max is having emergency surgery.

You call your folks, and your mother drives over to the hospital.

Finally the doctor comes to the waiting room and says Uncle Max will be fine in a few days. You're happy to hear the news and breathe a prayer of thanks.

THE END

Gloria frowns. "Why are people honking their horns?"

"Maybe they're celebrating. Let's go see what's happening."

She follows you, still sniffling. When you reach the car deck, you see a burly ferry worker holding a squirming boy under each arm. A man is standing beside a blue Ford. "I found them! They were asleep in my backseat."

"Your car is just like ours," Gloria exclaims.

Robby cries, "Bye-bye. Go bye-bye."

Bobby screams, "Bye-bye, Daddy's car."

"These your kids?" asks the attendant.

Gloria says, "Oh, yes. I'll take care of them." The man puts the boys down, and she squats down to hug them. "I've been so worried."

The ferry docks with a slight jolt, and the ferry worker removes the chains. You and Gloria lead the kids over to the stairway to get out of the way of the exiting cars. She keeps a firm grip on an arm of each boy.

Choices: You stay on the ferry (turn to page 63).
You decide to go ashore (turn to page 30).

"Not very good," Mother answers tearfully. "He got appendicitis when he was camping. His pain was so bad, he couldn't walk. He lay in his sleeping bag for two days and nights, hoping someone would find him. Poor Max."

You swallow hard. "I should have been there."

Your mother nods. "Maybe you could have found help for him before his appendix burst."

"Will he die?" you ask.

"We don't know yet."

You think, if he dies, it'll be my fault.

You sit around the hospital for hours. You feel as if you're in a hazy dream. But you're already awake.

Finally the doctor comes and tells you, "Max is going to be fine. He has a healthy body, and that's why he's coming through so well."

"Praise the Lord!" you exclaim. You're too happy to sit still. Might as well go outside and run around the hospital a few times to start your running program. Next time you go hiking with Uncle Max, you'll keep up with him.

THE END

You put on your backpack and start up the trail. You know you have a long hike ahead of you, but you hope you'll meet Uncle Max coming down.

Finally you reach a green lake. By then you're so hungry, you feel faint.

You see a man and woman roasting wieners over a small fire.

Choices: You keep going (turn to page 123).
You ask for food (turn to page 58).

You see a fellow strumming a guitar. No one pays much attention. You stop. His guitar case is open, and a lady tosses a coin in. You like to sing, and you recognize his songs from church. You say, "Maybe more people would listen if you had a singer."

He says, "Can't sing today. Got a sore throat."

"I'll sing if you want."

"Know 'Amazing Grace'? "

"Sure." You take a deep breath as he starts strumming the melody. You have to sing loudly to be heard above the market noise. Some people stop to listen and then drop coins into the case. Next you sing "How Great Thou Art" and "When the Saints Go Marching In."

A woman says, "God gave you a wonderful voice. Use it to praise him." She puts a dollar in the case.

When you finish a few more hymns, you say, "Got to go now. Let's split the money."

"Don't go yet. We make a good team."

"I gotta go home or my parents will get worried."

He takes the money and counts out half for you.

"Thanks." You have enough for the ferry fare and a snack. You say good-bye and hurry through the crowd. You wish you could earn money by doing something that's fun all the time.

THE END

While he's dialing, you run out the back door. You climb the man's wooden fence and run toward the road as fast as you can.

The man yells at you from his doorway. "Hey, come back here."

But you don't even turn. You run down the road until you get a pain in your side.

You stop, panting, and look back. You see a car backing out of the man's driveway. You can't outrun a car. You lie down flat in the wet drainage ditch and hope he won't see you.

The car goes by. You crawl under a barbwire fence and cross a field. You don't dare walk beside the road with that man looking for you.

You look at the paper in your hand. That's the license number of your kidnappers. You should give it to the sheriff, but you're afraid to talk to the sheriff. Maybe he won't believe you.

You go back to the resort and try to forget your scary time with Red and Joe. Maybe working for your parents isn't so bad after all.

THE END

Finally it begins to get dark again. Uncle Max still hasn't returned. He must have decided to stay another day.

You walk to the ranger station. It's scary walking along the road in the dark. You think you see animal eyes watching you. You run, and you're glad to see the lights of the building.

You call your dad and explain your problem.

Dad says, "Something must have happened to Max. He wouldn't leave you stranded. I'll be right over."

Dad comes and talks to the ranger who calls the Mountain Rescue Council. They organize a search to begin in the morning. Dad calls your church, and the pastor says he'll alert people to pray for Uncle Max.

The next day searchers start out for the Sapphire Lake area. You offer to go, too, but they tell you to stay at the ranger station where you'll hear all the news. In the afternoon, a searcher finds Uncle Max, and a helicopter takes him to the hospital.

Dad calls Mother, and then you and Dad drive to the hospital. Your heart is beating fast because you're worried about Uncle Max.

When you get to the hospital, you find your mother. "How is Uncle Max?" you ask.

Turn to page 82.

You sit on the float feeling depressed about the way things worked out. Suddenly a hairless head with large eyes breaks the surface.

You jump up screaming. "Zosta, is that you?"

"I'm answering your signal," she says.

"Just a minute." You run up to the dock and across the beach to the road where Mr. Wingle is getting into his car.

"Wait, wait," you shout. "Zosta is here. She wants to talk to you."

Mr. Wingle gets out of the car. "If you're playing a joke on me—" he begins.

"No, she's here. She really is."

Father and Mr. Wingle look skeptical, but they follow you back to the float.

"I don't see anything," complains Mr. Wingle.

You holler, "Zosta, we're here."

A head pops up beside the float, and Zosta climbs up and sits on the edge. Her fishlike face has a smile on it. She is wearing a metallic garment that looks like a swimsuit.

Mr. Wingle's mouth drops open as he stares at her.

Turn to page 70.

Finally the door opens a few inches, and you hear Brad whisper, "Hurry, before someone sees you."

You all slip inside.

Brad closes the door, but then you hear someone running down the hall. It's a tall man with muscular arms. "What do you kids think you're doing?" he hollers.

"Just looking for the rest rooms," lies Brad.

"You kids are sneaking in."

Brad pulls out his ticket stub. "Here's my ticket."

"How about the rest of you?"

"I lost mine," says Nora.

He glares at you, and then hollers, "Hey, Larry, we got some gate-crashers."

You feel your heart pounding. What's going to happen to you? The two little kids are crying.

Brad dashes for the door, but the man catches him and hauls him back. "I'm not through with you. I saw you open the door and let the other kids in."

Larry joins him, and they herd you into an office. Larry asks each of you your name, address, and telephone number.

The first man begins dialing.

Oh, no, they're calling your parents!

THE END

As you come to the car, Dad says, "Sorry you had to come all this way on a wild-goose chase."

Mr. Wingle laughs. "More like a wild-mermaid chase. Oh, well, it's a pretty spot. Wish I could stay longer, but our department is very busy."

He pats your head. "Don't let the mermaids kidnap you again."

You don't say anything. You feel you've let everyone down—the Ospians and mankind in general. Nobody believes what kids say. Someday everyone will be sorry, but then it will be too late. You wonder if you can find someone to help you build an ark.

THE END

You walk to town to the sheriff's office. You tell the sheriff the whole story, including the part about Tony's bribe.

He strokes his chin. "You ever been in trouble before?" he asks.

"No, sir." You pull out the paper where you wrote the license number of the kidnapper's truck. The sheriff mutters, "We've lost valuable time, but I'll alert the state patrol to watch for this truck."

You wait while he makes the call.

He looks at you with his steel gray eyes. "Remember, only bad guys have to fear the law. It protects the rest of us."

You nod. "May I go now?"

"Sure. When that kid comes to pick up his bribe money, remind him that bribery is a crime. He'll have to answer to me if he harasses you."

"Thanks a lot, Sheriff."

You jog home, a big load lifted from your shoulders.

THE END

Two fire engines and the sheriff's car roar by you with their sirens wailing. More cars follow. Some people can't resist going to a fire.

When you get there, you see a big hole where the dynamite shed used to be.

You stand around shivering while people talk excitedly. You walk up to the sheriff and tell him about your kidnapping.

He writes down your name and address. He says, "Those fellows won't be kidnapping any more kids or stealing any more dynamite."

"Are you sure they're dead?" you ask.

"Nobody could survive those explosions."

You think maybe if you had helped them, they'd still be alive, or maybe you'd be dead, too. You shudder.

The sheriff drives you home, and you tell your family about your adventures. Mom flutters around you and keeps saying, "Don't ever get in a strange car again."

You say, "I want to be a sheriff when I grow up. Maybe I could keep guys like Red and Joe from hurting people."

THE END

You say, "Hey, we can't go out there."

Gloria stands by the sign and calls, "Robby, Bobby, are you up here?"

"Come on, Gloria. I don't think they came here. The twins couldn't have caused the grounding. After all, they're only two," you tell her.

Gloria nods. "I just wish we'd find them. I can't understand where they could have gone."

You keep looking, and Gloria gets more and more distraught, for there's no sign of the boys.

The ship finally begins to move, and everyone seems happy except you and Gloria. You don't really want to go anywhere.

As you come closer to the city, you hear car horns beeping.

Turn to page 81.

Mr. Wingle leaves, and you wonder what is going to happen.

The next morning your dad gets a call from someone at the White House saying the president is coming to the resort that afternoon. You've never seen Dad so excited. Your parents run around cleaning and polishing everything. You can't really believe it's all happening.

As you walk up the road to mail some letters, a man gets out of a van and hollers, "Hey, kid, want to be on television?"

You feel excited. You remember Mr. Wingle's words that everything is top secret, but you may never have another chance to be on TV.

Choices: You run over to the van saying, "Sure" (turn to page 98).

You tell the man you don't want to be on TV (turn to page 102).

You don't feel any teeth. You turn your head and see the bear leaving. He's crashing through the brush. Maybe he didn't like the smell of the mosquito repellent you put on last night, or maybe he prefers raw fish to raw people.

You get up and start hiking, hoping you won't run into any more bears. You still haven't found a trail, and you're not even sure you're heading in the right direction. You think of Uncle Max. He's depending on you to get help, and you're lost. "Please, God. Help me," you pray.

You come to a river.

Choices: You follow the river (turn to page 107).
You retrace your steps, trying to find the trail (turn to page 74).

"How much?" you ask.

"Two seventy-five round trip," he says.

Gloria hands him her money. You give him your three dollars. He gives you tickets and a quarter in change.

You and Gloria run on the ferry and head for the upper deck. But the twins are no longer by the railing. "Where could they have gone?" mutters Gloria.

"They're here someplace. We'll search the boat until we find them."

Choices: You go to the coffee shop (turn to page 121).

You go to the car deck (turn to page 101).

By the time you reach the van, a cameraman has climbed out and is aiming his camera at you. The other fellow shakes your hand as he says, "We'd like to hear how you met the Ospians."

You smile and tell him about the storm and the bubble.

"But," interrupts your interviewer, "how did Washington get involved?"

"I don't think I'm supposed to talk about that."

"Why are officials trying to hide the facts?" he persists.

You squirm and try to think of an answer that won't get you in trouble. "They'll tell you everything at the right time."

"Is there a danger to the people? Is that the reason for the secrecy?" he demands.

"Not if we stop polluting the oceans. That's all the Ospians want." Then you realize you've said too much. "I didn't mean to say that."

"Thanks for the interview, kid."

They drive off, and you return to the lodge. You're worried that the president will be mad at you.

Choices: You decide to try to stop the station from running the tape (turn to page 112).

You go upstairs (turn to page 128).

You feel sorry for the young woman in the wheelchair, but the kid who took her purse is bigger than you. You hurry away. You don't like to see bad things happen. It makes you hurt inside. This isn't how you wanted to spend your day off.

THE END

As you run down the stairway to the lower deck, Gloria says, "The car deck is the most dangerous place because there's only a chain where the cars go on and off." She hurries to the bow of the ferry while you squirm between cars to the stern. There are no red jackets visible.

Then you look down, and your heart misses a beat. A piece of sugar cookie is lying on the deck. You look at the milky green froth churning in the boat's wake. If Robby and Bobby fell in that icy water . . .

Gloria joins you. "I don't see them here. We've got to get help."

You nod and point to the cookie piece. Gloria begins to cry. You say, "Don't fall apart, Gloria. Anybody could have dropped that cookie." You go back upstairs.

Turn to page 110.

Late in the afternoon, the president arrives by helicopter. He smiles and shakes your hand. "When do I meet the Ospian?"

You say, "I've already pushed the button. Zosta will come soon." You lead the president down the ramp to the float.

When Zosta's head appears, you call, "Zosta, the president of the United States is here to talk to you."

The president says, "I promise to do all I can to keep pollution from the ocean. I will request an emergency session of the United Nations to request cooperation from all nations."

Zosta answers, "I will tell the Ospian leaders that human beings are trying to stop water pollution. I am sure I can at least delay plans to drown land creatures."

Turn to page 103.

"We will do our best," promises the president.

Photographers take pictures of the president, Zosta, and you. Then Zosta slips back in the water, and the president shakes your hand and says good-bye. You watch the helicopter take off.

As you head back to the lodge, a plump fellow comes up to you. "Hey, kid, want a million dollars?"

You blink and stare at him. "What do I have to do?"

"Give me the little silver box."

"What are you going to do with it?"

"I just want to talk to this Ospian. With a million dollars you could buy everything you ever wanted."

Choices: You sell the box (turn to page 130).
You refuse (turn to page 119).

Very slowly you inch your way upward. You try not to think of the steep cliff below. A few windswept bushes serve as handholds. Your toes find cracks in the rock to use as precarious steps. Your left arm throbs painfully, and you hold it close to your chest. You use your right hand to hang on. You look up. Still a long way to go.

You reach for a bush. It comes up by the roots.

You fall into space. You fling out your arms trying to grab something, but you feel only air— until the crash.

Pain thunders through your body.

Darkness . . . nothing . . . .

THE END

The road is just two tracks, partly grown over with weeds. After hours of walking, you come to the highway.

When you finally find a gas station, you call the sheriff and describe your experiences and give him the truck license number.

"We'll find them," says the sheriff confidently. "They must be the fellows who blew up the Conedale Bank last month."

"They said they had to hurry to do a job. I hope you find them before they blow up somebody."

"I'll send out an alert to the law enforcement agencies."

He hangs up, and you call your dad to come and pick you up.

Late that night you hear this flash on the radio: "Two men were arrested as they tried to blow up the Oakville Bank. A policeman recognized the license number of their truck. It was reported by a kid who was kidnapped by the pair."

You say to yourself, "I'm glad that's over."

But it isn't completely over. The next day a reporter comes to interview you and take your picture. When the story comes out in the paper, some kids from school stop by to see you.

One says, "Weren't you scared?"

You shake your head. But friendships shouldn't start with lies. You admit, "I was terrified out of my skull."

THE END

You go on home, feeling miserable. Later that afternoon, Tony comes to the resort, and you hand him the forty dollars you've been saving so long. You feel a big lump in your throat. You try to swallow, and you say in a choked voice, "You won't tell anyone at school that I'm a thief, will you?"

"I said I'd help you escape from the sheriff. If you want me to keep quiet at school, I'll need more money."

"I don't have any more."

"By September you can get more. Your dad must be rich to own a place like this."

"He's not rich and we all work hard. I won't pay you any more money."

"I'll tell everyone you help crooks."

Tony leaves. You feel a hard knot in your stomach. You wish you had never promised to pay Tony. You should have depended on the truth to keep you out of trouble.

THE END

Part of the time you have to walk in the water because the vegetation along the bank is too thick to walk through. Water squishes in your boots, and your feet feel as if they've been stored in the freezer, but you keep going.

Finally you see a fisherman standing in the river. You call, "Where's the campground?"

He points downstream. "Keep going until you come to a bridge."

"Thanks." You keep sloshing along until the underbrush thins out so you can walk along the bank. When you come to a footbridge, you cross it.

Turn to page 80.

"Nobody important will listen to a kid," you explain.

Zosta goes away, as if she's angry. You sit in your bubble prison while various Ospians swim by and stare at you. From the way they're gesturing and laughing, you must be the funniest creature they've ever seen.

You wish there were a way to escape. There's a trapdoor at the top of the bubble, but even if you could push it open, the water would drown you. You often wondered how your goldfish feel. Now, you know.

THE END

You feel very important. Everyone in the whole country will hear about you and see your picture. You're happy about being famous, especially when people offer you money just for using your picture or your name. Maybe people will write to you and ask for your picture and autograph as they do movie stars.

Mom interrupts your thoughts. "I need help cleaning cabins. Every one is reserved for tonight."

"You don't mean me?"

"Of course I mean you. Who else will help me?"

You can't think of a good answer to that so you get the cleaning cart. Being famous doesn't do much good at home.

THE END

Suddenly you hear a loud scraping noise, and the ferry lurches and stops. You sit down on the floor—hard. People scream. Everybody talks at once.

"What happened?"

"Must've hit another ship."

"Will we sink?"

A man opens a chest of life jackets and hands them out. You scramble up and grab two—one for Gloria and one for you. If the boat's sinking, you want to be prepared.

Then a voice comes over the loudspeaker. "Attention, all passengers. There is no danger. We have temporarily run aground, but we'll soon be floating again. Remain calm. We'll be a little off schedule, but you'll all arrive in the city safely."

Gloria dumps her life jacket on a bench. "I wonder why the ship went aground." She frowns.

You say, "Are you thinking what I'm thinking you're thinking?"

You both race outside and up the stairs to the top deck. A sign across the top of the stairway reads NO ADMITTANCE.

Choices: You keep going (turn to page 127).
You obey the sign (turn to page 94).

You ride your bike into town, pedaling as fast as you can. You decide to go to Judge Falkin's office. Maybe he can issue a court order stopping the TV station from showing the tape. There should be time before the evening news.

As you come to the outskirts of town, you see Marty, a kid from school, but you don't stop.

But Marty yells, "Hey, I just saw you on TV!"

You brake fast. Marty runs over to you. "Tell me about these Oxians."

"Ospians. Did they show me talking to the TV man?"

"Yeah, they interrupted Mom's soap opera. She was mad, but I said, 'That's a kid from school.' They zoomed right in on your face. I couldn't believe it. Wow! Hey, did you see yourself?"

You shake your head. "I better get home," you say. There's no use talking to Judge Falkin now.

When you get home, a Secret Service agent scolds you for talking to the TV reporter. She says the president is coming to see Zosta, and they have to provide a lot more security now that the news was on TV.

You're sorry there is no way to take back your words.

Turn to page 102.

"I won't pay you any money," you tell Tony, even though you're scared of what's going to happen to you.

Tony shrugs. "Don't say I didn't try to help."

Soon you hear the siren of the sheriff's car. The sheriff comes in the house, and you retell your story, showing him the truck's license plate number. He believes you. "I'll radio the state patrol to set up roadblocks. What'd the crooks look like?"

"One was bald, and the other guy had red hair," you answer.

"We know who they are. And with an eyewitness to testify, we'll get a conviction."

You ride back to town with the sheriff, and he explains the procedure he follows when there's a crime. When you get to headquarters, a reporter is waiting for you. He takes your picture and asks a bunch of questions.

Your parents are really surprised when they see your picture in the paper the next day. The story tells how your information helped the sheriff catch the crooks. Dad cuts it out and puts it on the bulletin board at the lodge. "That's my kid," he tells everyone.

People keep asking you questions about your adventure. You shrug. "It's just one of those things that happen."

THE END

The young woman leads the way to the aquarium. You're glad to see a policeman standing near the entrance. The tough guys disappear. She says, "I have half an hour left on my lunch hour. My name's Jan, and I'll give you a quick tour."

You look at lots of fascinating fish, but your favorite exhibit is the sea otters. They swim around as if they're entertaining an audience. Jan knows all their names.

Jan shows you salmon fingerlings and explains, "They'll be released in the sound to swim to the ocean and then return here in a few years to lay their eggs."

"How do they know their way back?" you ask.

"God gave them a special sense for finding their way to their spawning ground without maps or direction signs." She looks at her watch. "I have to get back to my job. I'm a ticket seller, but I'm studying to be a marine biologist."

"Thanks for the tour."

"Thanks for my purse." Jan steers her wheelchair toward the entrance. You wander around looking at the fish.

You think, God must have a great sense of humor to make so many funny fish—but a wolf eel probably looks gorgeous to another wolf eel.

THE END

You enjoy browsing in the little shops containing a variety of handcrafted and secondhand items. Then you come to open stalls where vendors are selling fresh vegetables and fruits. You squirm through the crowds who are looking for bargains. Seeing all the food makes you hungry, and you look longingly at the small restaurants you pass.

You don't have any money, so your complaining stomach will have to wait until you get home. You reach in your jacket pocket for your ferry ticket. You keep feeling around, but all you find is a hole. Your ticket is gone! Your stomach cramps into a painful spasm.

Choices: Call your parents (turn to page 77).
Try to earn some money (turn to page 84).

You wake up as the sun is coming up, and you remember you're a long way from anyone you know or from any food. The blisters on your feet protest, but you start toward the ridge. There's a great hollow where your stomach is, but you try to ignore it.

You reach the ridge and cross a snowfield. The glare hurts your eyes, and you're weak from hunger. You slip on the snow. You try to catch yourself as you slide down the snowbank, but you keep sliding. Ouch! Your battered body stops as you hit a large rock.

Your hands are bleeding, and you feel pain from your head to your toes. You look around and see that below you is a steep cliff. The big rock kept you from going over. You don't dare move for fear of dislodging the rock.

You shiver, and tears roll down your cheeks. You holler, "HELP! HELP!" but there is no one to hear. You wonder if you'll still be here when it gets dark and cold. Someday someone may find your frozen body.

Choices: You lie still (turn to page 68).
You try to crawl up the mountain (turn to page 104).

You see Gloria get on the ferry, but you think the twins must be in town somewhere. Lots of little kids have red jackets. You walk up and down the street peering in the stores, looking for signs of chaos. The ferry leaves.

You finally stop looking. The twins aren't your responsibility, and someone will certainly find them.

Choices: You go home (turn to page 138).
You stay in town (turn to page 50).

You hike back to the car. It has started to rain, and you're getting soaked. The car is locked. You wish you had asked Uncle Max for his keys.

You walk to the campgrounds. All the campers are in their tents or trailers. You hear kids laughing, and you feel lonely.

You crawl under a picnic table where it's fairly dry. You wish you had stayed with Uncle Max. Hunger pangs are getting worse, and even his liver and spinach burgers would taste good. You eat a candy bar, but you're still hungry.

When it gets dark, you roll out your sleeping bag under the table, but you don't sleep much. Gnats crawl on your face, and the bites itch.

The next day you slowly eat your sack of peanuts. Your food is gone. You wait and wait for Uncle Max to come back to his car, but he doesn't come. By late afternoon you're boiling mad. Why isn't Uncle Max back? He knows you can't go home until he gets here.

Choices: You decide to walk up the trail to meet him (turn to page 83).
You keep waiting (turn to page 87).

You shake your head. "I can't sell the silver box. It's the only way to summon the Ospians, and that's important for our country and for the world."

"Think of what you could do with a million dollars. You'd be rich for life," he whispers.

"I won't sell the box, so you're wasting your time." You walk away, but he follows you.

"How about two million?"

"No!"

"You're crazy, kid. You could travel around the world. You're turning down the chance of a lifetime."

You run toward the lodge. You don't like this fellow. You're not sure what he's up to, but you don't trust him. You decide to ask your dad to put the silver box in the safe.

At the lodge you find other people waiting to see you. Several TV stations ask for interviews. An author wants to write the story of your life. A T-shirt company wants permission to put your picture on a T-shirt. A cereal company and a hamburger chain ask you to endorse their products.

Choices: You sign all the contracts (turn to page 109).

You say you want to talk to your parents (turn to page 124).

You stammer, "I—I thought you didn't want that wallet. Why'd you throw it on the closet floor if you wanted it?"

The girl begins to cry.

One of her brothers hoots, "Why would anybody cry about a picture of a nerd like Alex?"

The man turns to your mother. "I hope you'll fire this no-good cabin cleaner who tried to steal my daughter's money."

You wish you could disappear. Mother looks at you as if she's very disappointed. You say, "I'll go through the dumpster. I'll find the wallet."

"We'll mail it to you," promises Mother.

The girl takes her twenty dollars from her father and barks at you, "You'd better find Alex's picture or we'll tell everybody what a gyp joint this is."

"Gyp joint, gyp joint," chant the little kids as they are herded back into the car.

You put on your oldest clothes and spend the rest of the day sorting through garbage—rotten food, used diapers, all kinds of smelly, awful stuff.

Finally you find the wallet. You wipe off the guck and look at Alex's picture. He has a fat face, stringy hair, and a silly expression. You went through torture for that dumb picture.

THE END

As you and Gloria come into the restaurant, you see a man mopping up a mess on the floor.

Gloria asks, "Have you seen two little boys in red jackets?"

He glares at you. "You mean the red tornadoes? They roared through here a few minutes ago. People who were carrying food to the tables didn't have a chance. The tornadoes ran into them. Hamburgers, coffee, sodas, doughnuts all went flying. Look at this mess I gotta clean up."

"Let's get out of here," whispers Gloria. You go to a quieter area where people are sitting on benches—reading, talking, or looking at the scenery.

Turn to page 110.

Joe pushes you into the one-room cabin. It smells musty, and you cough from the dust disturbed by your feet. There's a wood-burning range and a sink with no faucets. You look around noting the lack of plumbing and electricity. You don't want to stay here.

Joe takes down a rope that's hanging on a nail. Red steers you over to the narrow cot in one corner and pushes you down. He holds you while Joe ties your hands together and then ties your ankles as well.

"Why are you tying me up? I helped you, didn't I?"

"We don't want you blabbing about stuff," says Red.

"I won't tell anyone. I promise. You can't leave me here to starve," you cry.

"We'll send you a pizza." Red laughs, as if whether you live or die is a big joke.

Joe slams the door, and you hear a key click in the lock.

You keep twisting your hands, trying to loosen the rope with your fingers, but your wrists soon begin to smart where the rough rope rubbed the skin off. You haven't been able to loosen a single knot. They've left you here to die. Tears flow down your face.

Turn to page 78.

When you get to the high alpine country, you see green meadows and snow-covered peaks, but mostly you're thinking of your stomach. You wonder if any of the plants are edible, but you don't dare eat any, because lots of plants are poisonous.

You finally come to a small blue lake. The sign says it is Sapphire Lake. But Uncle Max is not here.

The sun has dropped behind the mountains, and a cold wind blows from the glaciers. Soon it will be dark, and there is no time to hike back to the campground. You crawl into your sleeping bag, and the warmth feels good. But your stomach is still sending frantic signals. You keep thinking of hamburgers, pizza, and apple pie. Even liver and spinach would taste good—anything to take away the awful gnawing emptiness.

Finally you go to sleep. You dream you're sitting down to Thanksgiving dinner, but an earthquake makes the table of food disappear in a big crack in the earth. You wake up hungrier than ever. It takes a long time to go back to sleep.

Choices: **Keep on reading (turn to page 116).**
Go to the kitchen for a snack (in case you're hungry). Then turn to page 116.

You tell your parents, "I don't like all this stuff. I'm just an ordinary kid. I don't want people staring at me when I walk down the street."

Dad says, "You're famous because you discovered the Ospians. But you don't have to go on TV or let them put your picture on T-shirts."

"Yeah, I want to downplay this so the kids at school won't think I'm trying to be some kind of superstar."

Dad strokes his chin. "This is going to be good for our resort business. I'm going to build more cabins—no, I think I'll build a big hotel. Tourists will want to stay at the place where the president talked to the Ospians."

You frown. "If a lot of people come, there'll be more work."

Mom says, "I'm going to hire help. Then I'll tell other people what to do."

You smile. "Maybe I won't have to clean messy cabins much longer."

"Maybe not," agrees Mom. "A hotel will need a bellhop to carry luggage and run errands. I'll buy you a classy uniform."

You groan. You'll look like a freak dressed in a fancy suit.

THE END

You say to the girl, "Better start bailing, or we might sink."

She looks scared again. She picks up a coffee can and starts to bail water from the bottom of the boat.

Then you see she's crying. "Hey, don't cry. We'll make it," you say with more bravery than you feel.

Finally you get out of the channel, and the rowing is easier, although you're still battling high waves. It's raining hard, and rainwater is collecting in the boat. You're very glad when you finally reach your float.

You call the other resort, and the girl's father comes to get her. He scowls at his daughter. "I told you not to go out alone," he barks. "Your mother has been frantic!" He looks at you. "You the one who rescued her?"

You nod.

He pulls ten dollars from his wallet and hands it to you. "Our daughter is worth a lot more than that, but it shows we're thankful for what you did."

"You don't have to pay me."

But he insists you take the money. "We love our daughter even if she does get herself in a lot of scrapes."

She smiles at you. "I want to be brave like you when I get big."

THE END

Granny fixes you a cup of hot cocoa, and you eat her spicy cookies while she talks and talks.

"I remember the first radio we had. I was excited when my husband put the earphones of that old crystal set on my head, and I heard singing. 'Where does the sound come from?' I asked. He tried to explain it, but I never could understand.

"You young folks take all these things for granted. The farm where I grew up didn't have electricity. My mother cooked on a wood stove and heated water for washing on that stove. If someone had told us that someday we could buy a box that would show moving pictures from all over the world and even the moon, we'd have thought he was addled in the head."

Granny stops for breath, and you say, "I think I better go."

Granny looks out the window. "Bad storm out there. Why don't you wait until it stops raining?"

You listen to Granny talk about the good old days until the rain stops pounding the roof. Then you leave.

When you come back later with the batteries, Granny's wrinkled face lights up. "Praise the Lord, I'll be able to hear God's good news on my radio."

THE END

You crawl under the chain with the NO ADMITTANCE sign. A crew member runs over. "No passengers on this deck," he snaps.

Gloria explains, "We're looking for my little brothers. Have you seen two little boys dressed in red?"

The crewman growls, "I didn't see them, but the captain did. They walked right into the wheelhouse. While Captain Archer was trying to get one kid away from his navigational instruments, the other boy tried to swing on the wheel. Those wild kids made us go aground."

"But where are they?" demanded Gloria.

"I don't know what happened to them after Captain Archer told them to get out of the wheelhouse."

"May we look around?"

"I suppose so. Just don't go near the wheelhouse. The captain's in a terrible mood. He's trying to explain to his superiors how he happened to run aground."

You and Gloria look around the top deck, but there's no sign of the twins. Gloria says, "I'm going to talk to the captain."

You swallow hard. "I don't want to face a captain in a terrible mood."

"He's the only one who can help us."

Choices: You shake your head and go below (turn to page 76).

You go with Gloria (turn to page 59).

You go to the family room and turn on TV. You start watching an old "Star Trek" episode, hoping it will make you forget your worries. But it's interrupted for a special news report. It's your interview! You feel sick to your stomach.

Soon everyone will know about the Ospians.

Dad calls you downstairs. Secret Service agents have arrived, and they announce the president is coming.

A woman with piercing brown eyes scowls at you. "You've made our job harder by spouting off to TV. Reporters and curiosity seekers will swarm around this resort."

You gulp. "I'm sorry."

Another agent says, "We better call the state patrol and tell them to send more help. We must make the resort safe for the president."

Even though the resort's closed, throngs of people gather by the fence trying to see what's going on. Boaters begin to converge on the resort from the bay, and the Coast Guard is called to keep them away from the float where Zosta is expected.

You're sorry you had a part in spreading the story. You hope the president doesn't scold you.

Turn to page 102.

You hurry as you think how good it'll feel to be warm and dry again. You figure that Joe's ax must have shaken up the dynamite. From the size of the explosions, you guess there's nothing left of the shed or Joe and Red.

Clouds have hidden the bright morning sun. It's starting to rain, but you can't get any wetter than you already are.

Your mom scolds you for going off and for getting your clothes so wet. "I didn't realize it was raining that hard," she says. But she's so busy scolding you, she forgets to ask where you've been.

You don't tell her you swam across a pond to get away from kidnappers. You don't want to admit you got into a stranger's vehicle when she's always warned you not to do that.

THE END

A million dollars will make you and your family rich. You could stop working and have fun!

You pull the silver box from your pocket and hand it to the man. He gives you a check for a million dollars.

You run to your dad and show him the check.

He frowns. "You shouldn't have sold the box. What if the president comes back and wants to talk to Zosta?"

Your mother adds, "You don't even know if this check is good. Why didn't you talk it over with us before you did such a foolish thing? Who was this man?"

"He gave me his card." You pull the card from your pocket and read, "James Rolliver, owner of Amazing Aquarium. Oh, no! I bet he wants to catch an Ospian for his aquarium! He'll make the Ospians so mad they're sure to flood the earth!"

THE END

You investigate the door carefully. As long as you can't break down the door, you'll have to work on the lock.

You take the paring knife and insert it between the door and the doorframe, trying to push back the bolt that locks the door. It moves a little but not enough.

You look to see if you can find a better tool. You find a metal skewer, and this gives you an idea. You push back the bolt with the knife. Then you hold it in that position with the skewer as you push again with the knife. On the third try, you hear the lock pop.

You can open the door.

You rush out, breathing the fresh air. Even the rain that is now falling feels good after that musty cabin. You're free although you're a long way from civilization. You start walking down the logging road.

Turn to page 105.

The vegetable soup tastes good, but you feel funny about pretending you're poor.

Norm says, "These people keep feeding me. They figure one of these days I'll come to Bible club, too."

"Aren't you interested in what the Bible has to say?"

"Naw, it's a rule book. I don't like rules. I want to have fun."

"Hey, God wants us to be happy."

"You a Christian?" he asks.

"Sure. Jesus pulls things together so life makes sense."

He shrugs. "How come you ran away from home?"

"I didn't run away. I just came to visit, and I got stuck with no money. I'm going home tonight."

"I could go home, but Mom yells at me all the time."

"Isn't it scary living on the streets?"

Turn to page 79.

As you walk home it starts to rain hard, and you run. At home you make yourself a peanut-butter-and-jelly sandwich. Mom comes in when she finishes waiting on a customer in the store.

You tell her about Gloria. "It doesn't seem fair that she has to take care of those two kids every day of her vacation."

Your mother looks at you. "Children who learn responsibility early have an easier time when they grow up."

"Is that what you're trying to do—teach me responsibility?" You wrinkle your nose.

"Yes, and we need your help. Next time you feel you need a day off, I hope you'll talk to me about it. I really missed you this morning. We lost some customers who didn't want to wait for me to clean a cabin for them."

"I didn't have much fun," you admit. "But cleaning cabins is gross."

She smiles. "Happiness comes from the right balance of work and play. If you play all the time, you soon get bored."

Not much chance of that happening around here.

THE END

You decide you don't like this part of town. You hurry back to the ferry terminal to wait for the next ferry. You look at the schedule. It's an hour before the ferry leaves. You sit on a bench and think about Mom's fried chicken and chocolate cake. You can't wait to get home, even though you know Mom's going to say, "Where have you *been* all day?"

THE END

You plead, "Mr. Wingle, listen. The Ospians are not Russians. I saw hundreds of them swimming in the water."

Mr. Wingle shrugs. "It's impossible for them to melt the polar ice caps."

"But what if you're wrong? Think of how many people could drown. Please, come back and talk to Zosta again."

"My boss will think I'm nuts."

"But if the ocean waters start rising, he'll remember the threat he sent you to investigate."

Slowly Mr. Wingle turns around and walks back to the dock. You push the red button. Finally Zosta pokes her head up from the water. "Have you decided you believe me?"

Mr. Wingle answers, "I'm not sure."

Zosta laughs, a deep, rumbling laugh. "If you ignore my request, you will drown. Tell your president we can help one another. We can replace your primitive engines with machines that do not need fuel. Then you will no longer spill oil in our oceans."

"The president would like to know about that."

Zosta says, "I will return home now. Buzz me when you can promise us clean water."

Mr. Wingle says, "I'll go back and report this to Washington. Until I get further instructions, we'll treat it as top secret."

Turn to page 95.

You want to go where the purse snatcher and his tough friends can't find you. You run back to the ferry terminal as fast as you can.

By the time you get there, you're out of breath, and your heart is pounding. You keep looking around to see if the tough kids followed you.

"Bummer," you mutter as you board the ferry. "Some day off."

THE END

Mom scolds you for going off without telling her. Then she says, "Maybe we have been working you too hard, but there's so much to do. How would you like Tuesday off every week?"

"That would be great, but you and Dad never take any time off."

"If things work out the way we've planned, we'll be able to hire some help by next summer." Mom hurries toward the door with a load of clean linen for a cabin.

You think about what you'll do on your next day off. Maybe you'll take a ferry to the city—or row over to Agate Island and look for treasure—or walk to town and look for a new friend.

THE END